Inverted Paradise

Lenny Hamilton is out of work, a doormat-type personality, chased by a clinging needy-type girl. He was in a sad state when he got a phone call from a friend, son of a major mobster. Marko Ponti was trying to get away from the mobster lifestyle and had taken on a job, housewatching a mansion on a tropical Caribbean island, all expenses paid for two people! Would Lenny like to be the second person?

What? You're kidding, right?

PA:

A man is offered a vacation on a tropical island, all expenses paid. He arrives and is met with a fantastic tropical island peopled by physical gods and goddesses in a society that seems made for paradise.

Why is he there at all? What is behind strange happenings? How has he changed? What does his companion's gangster father have to do with it?

What happens if this paradise turns into an inverted paradise?

***½

Contents

About the author

CD Moulton has traveled extensively over much of the world both in the music business, where he was a rock guitarist, songwriter and arranger and in an import/export business. He has been everything from a bar owner to auto salvage (junkyard) manager, longshoreman to high steel worker, orchid grower to landscaper, tropical fish farmer to commercial fisherman. He started writing books in 1983 and has published more than 350 books as of January 1, 2023. His most popular books to date are about research with orchids, though much of his science fiction and fantasy work has proven popular. He wrote the CD Grimes, PI series, and the Det. Nick Storie series, Clint Faraday series, and many other works.

He now resides in Gualaca, Chiriqui, Panamá, where he writes books, plays music with friends, does research with orchids and medicinal plants. He has lately become involved in fighting for the rights of the indigenous people, who are among his closest friends, and in fighting the extreme corruption in the courts and police in Panamá.

He offers the free e-book, *Fading Paradise*, that explains what he has been through because of the corruption.

CD is the discoverer of the Chadam Protocol for curing cancer.

Facebook page Ambrosia peruviana for cancer.

Inverted Paradise

Blue Thursday

Sometimes you wake up in the morning, full of energy and ready to face the day. Sometimes you don't. Sometimes you wake up with a strong premonition that says you'd be wise to just stay in bed and wait for tomorrow.

Lenny Hamilton had far too many of those.

What the hell!

He got up and stumbled into the bathroom for the morning things. When he looked in the mirror, he made a wry grimace and swore. He looked like he felt. Like a leftover pizza with a warm beer.

He got back in the shower and turned it all the way over to cold.

It was hardly even cool. Shit!

He went back into the room and turned on the (Not allowed here!) coffee pot to heat up yesterday's leftover mud. He waited until it was hot, then unplugged it and took out the hidden hotplate from under the table and put a pan with two cups of water in it onto the coil. He flipped on the TV and watched a couple of minutes of what was passing for news today. It was the same as had passed for news yesterday and the day before. An idiot sexy woman in a tight dress was telling about a wreck where four small children and their parents were killed when a rock truck hit them – with a bright empty smile on her face.

"Stupid silly dumb bitch! You don't do the studio empty smile when you're reporting a goddamned *tragedy*!" he snarled at the screen.

Hell! She must have heard him! She suddenly dropped the smile and tried for a compassionate look, but couldn't quite manage that, so went for an interested look that didn't quite fit, either.

Lenny wondered if anyone else in a city of two hundred thousand people even noticed.

He opened the dry starchy noodles and dumped them into the now-hot water. The flavor package dropped out with the noodles, so he fished it out with his only spoon and tossed it into the trash.

The phone rang. He let it, then picked it up when he saw it wasn't going to stop.

"Hi! Lisa here! How're you feeling this bright morning?"

Lisa Fischer. Pain-in-the-ass clinger type. Not too bad-looking and would have a decent personality if she'd drop the needy part.

"Oh. Hi, Lee. I'm in a very bad mood, so beware! I haven't had my coffee yet!"

She laughed. "I'm going to Dan's party tonight and wheedled an invite for you, so we can go about sevenish."

How nice of you to let me know how you've made a date with you for me! he thought.

"Gee, Lee. I wish you'd let me know yesterday. I can't possibly make it tonight. I've got a job for a couple of nights and really do have to make enough for the rent next week," he lied. "Dan and I don't get along, so I won't be missed. Maybe Frank can go in my place. He sort of likes you."

Frank Beresford was another pain-in-the-ass. They'd make a pair!

She radiated disappointment over the phone. "Oh, Len! I worked so hard to ... well ... maybe we can see each other this afternoon and make it another day, huh?"

"I have to see the lawyer this morning about that bad check I got from Harvey. He's got my laptop and I've got a bouncer. He says tough shit, put it through again and maybe it'll pass. He gets away with that crap with a lot of people. He's not getting away with it with me!"

"Can't you bring charges with the police for that?"

"They won't be able to locate him. His crooked brother-in-law is dispatcher at the station, and calls him when they send the car to pick him up so he can be elsewhere. John, Sam, and Jan have all been through that. They told me not to take his check, right there, and I said there were other ways to collect on a check that didn't bring relatives into it.

"Look, Lee. I'll call you as soon as I get away from the shyster. That's assuming I can get away from him early enough to where I can meet you, of course. You know how lawyers are."

"Yeah. I had an appointment with one two months ago, at ten in the morning, and couldn't even get to see her until after three! I really should have gotten up and walked out!"

Except you like being walked on, he thought. "Ain't *that* the truth! I'll see if I can get away at a reasonable hour."

"Okay. I'll be waiting with bated breath! Ciao!"

Lenny hung up and ran a hand through his thick brown hair that needed cutting, took the forty cent breakfast off the hotplate, dumped in the can of Vienna sausages, added a shot of catsup, and swore at his being as bad as her. He should get the spine to tell her to flake off!

The phone rang again. He sighed and picked it up. She'd call ten times, probably.

"Len? Marko here. I've got a deal I think you'll really like! It'll be like a paid vacation for us!"

"What's this one about, Marko?" Marko kept coming up with deals. Most of them were ways for his mobster family to get him out of their hair for a month or two, and the strings were too confining, even though the "deal" was usually tempting. Lenny met him five years ago, and they got along semi-well, then, about four or five months ago, they were at a party and met. Marko was dating a beautiful girl who had a sister there without a date. She was as beautiful, and Marko introduced Lenny to Gloria. They hit it off, and went doubles for a few dates. Marko and Lenny seemed to have a lot in common, and got closer. He soon learned how Marko's father was an enormously powerful gangster boss, and that Marko wanted nothing more in life than to escape that situation and the family reputation. They shared friends and interests on the internet chats. Lenny introduced some net friends, and Marko introduced some.

"This one's different! (They were all "different" – in the telling). It's not about Pops trying to get me away from his lovely 'business' dealings. It's a housesitting deal on a Caribbean island. The people who own the place want someone there for four months while they do a tour of Europe. Everything's paid, and we get a hundred twenty five a week apiece. We have a charge account for groceries and that kind of thing, and for gas for the boat – there's a thirty two foot fishing boat, and a ski boat, and jet skis, and a lot of other stuff. We have a Porsche to drive, and two ATVs.

"It's perfect! It doesn't have anything the least crooked in it! Pops doesn't even know the people.!"

"How did you find out about it?"

"Through you, actually. The net. I was on a chat at a forum. We'd been chatting for a long time. I didn't know anything about them, except they weren't in the states. They'd hinted about being in the Caribbean, but I thought on the mainland, in Costa Rica, or maybe Nicaragua. It's an island, down around there, but a hundred miles from the mainland. The pictures look like Tahiti or one of those dream vacation places.

"The Howards. You sent them to me on the net. You chatted a lot with her because of the driftwood thing you and Moms do.

"Come on, Len! We get along. This will be a flyer that could be really awesome!"

He thought about it. "I think ... why the hell not? If I can get the four hundred Harvey owes me for his bad check, I can swing it."

"I'll get your money from that scrud! We can leave Saturday. I have the tickets reserved. Everything's paid for. Pack light. How says all you'll need is a bathing suit, and even that's optional!"

"Hmm. I'll have to get my passport renewed, I suppose. I haven't used it, except once, five or six years ago. We'll have to go to their embassy or whatever to get a visa."

"Nope! All handled right there on the island. We can go stay at one of Pops' places in Miami until Saturday. We can leave here as soon as you want."

Well, Lisa wants me to call her this afternoon. I can't if I'm on my way to Miami! "How about, say, four o'clock?"

"Today?"

"Too soon?"

"No way! Make it three thirty!"

"Done!"

He had to be totally insane to even consider this!

He called Lisa, and said he only had ten seconds. He had to leave the country! Right now! Work. He couldn't pass this opportunity. Call when I can. Ciao!

He started packing some things and cleaning the place. The rent was paid, despite what he told Lisa, for seven more months.

He had to be crazy! He didn't do things like this!

The phone rang. "Lenny? This is Harvey Pitner. I, er, I'm sending the cash over for the check. I really shouldn't do that to people. I'm sorry. It won't happen again. I added a bit for interest.

"You know Marko Ponti? He's having his, er, friend bring you the money.

"I really sincerely apologize for this."

"It's in the past. I'm going on my vacation, and really do need the money. Thanks."

He hung up. Marko's friend?

He had just finished packing and straightening things up when there was a knock. He opened the door, and a huge, what he could only label as a goon, stood there.

"You Len?"

"Uh, yeah?"

"Here." He handed Len five hundred dollar bills. "Marko wants me to wait and drive you to the place so you can go to the airport or whatever."

"Come on in. I'm almost ready."

"Yeah. Okay. I'm Thor."

Brother, does the name fit! "I've got a little stale coffee, if you want it."

"Yeah. Okay."

He barely fit through the doorway. There wasn't a bit of fat on him. He was just big and mean-looking.

After about twenty minutes, Lenny took his bags to the waiting car, a Mercedes, and left the keys to his place with Ms. Ames, the landlady.

He got in the car. As soon as Thor started the engine, he told himself, *The adventure begins! I'm totally insane, but I think everybody should do something unbelievably stupid once in their lifetime!*

Lenny and Marko got on the small jet island-hopper in a light drizzle in Kingston, Jamaica. This was the first time Lenny had been outside the states, except the one time to Canada, and that was hardly a difference. The noise and colors were fascinating, as were the happy people with their strange, to him, customs.

They'd stayed in Kingston the night before. Marko spoke a little Spanish, which wasn't needed, though he said it might be needed on the island they were going to inhabit. He also spoke French and German, which surprised Lenny, but his father was an international gangster with villas almost everywhere, if the local scuttle could be believed. Lenny could get along okay in Spanish. There were a lot of people from Puerto Rico around where he grew up.

That was the first night he spent in a brothel, too. He had a very good time, but wasn't easy in the atmosphere. Marko took it as a matter of course. They both got a little drunk, but were up and ready when their island hopper took them aboard at nine thirty. They were the only two passengers, and the pilot explained that it was chartered. The place they were going was private property, and the airfield was used by private planes, almost exclusively.

There was a moment when the plane seemed to bounce upward, then to fall a few hundred feet. The pilot explained that it was an inversion, then had to lecture about how the air currents could suddenly change direction. It was flowing downward from a small dome of high pressure, then was suddenly reversed, flowing upward from a corresponding low. They were common, in some areas, because of the different temperatures in major ocean currents. A cold stream caused a downward flow, and a warmer one caused it to flow upward.

"It's inversion, which means to turn upside-down. They're small here, and don't form a shear force, which is a strong channel of air flow, generally spoken of if it's from one side or the other."

"Sheez! All I did was say that was quite a bounce!" Marko exclaimed. They laughed about it.

They were shown which island it was from ten thousand feet. The pilot flew over and circled as he descended, then called on a special channel on the radio to announce it was a flight bringing guests of the Howards. Permission to land was granted, and they went in. The pilot explained that to land there without permission was dangerous. The people might think he was a drug runner or something, and would shoot him down. The island was isolated, to a great degree, and the people there were so adamant about keeping the drug trade off the island the US Coast Guard didn't even pay attention to it. The way the US tried to run all the countries down there, that said a hell of a lot!

"Everyone in the world knows the politicians in the US are behind ninety percent of the drug trade, and are just manipulating their own people and the Latin American countries with that shit. The people here are mostly from the US, and are really rich, so they tell those crooked slimy leeches exactly where their asshole is (Marko later explained that the local expression was, 'He's too stupid to know where his asshole is') when they try to tell them what to do. I wish a lot more would tell those lying scumballs where to get off!"

Lenny was a bit shocked, but Marko seemed used to it, to the point he agreed.

"You need Bill Clinton. Gringos were liked all over the world until King Dubya tried to dictate to everybody. Now you're not welcome, most places. Be glad we know it's not the people, it's just their damned shithead politicians. Some cousins of the Bushes or something had a place here. He was told it might be a good idea if he sold it to some human beings, that fatuous pigs weren't welcome on Isla Tintada.

"That's what they called them. Fatuous pigs. The Bushes had a lot of money, but not even a drop in the ocean to what some of these people have. Most of them are really good people, but a couple are, as one of the snotty type said about the native people, 'rather trying.' That one's from England, not the states. They don't have a clue as to how to treat anyone not in their 'social class, don't you know, old sock.'

"Well, you have the code at the house to call me if you need anything. It's paid for, whatever. I sometimes bring over a few packages from the supermarkets in Kingston. Two grand to take them fifty bucks worth of groceries! It must be nice! I don't get too many passengers out here. You're only the second and third in a month. Other was a knockout woman going to visit some of the natives. She seemed to have plenty of money. No native could afford me!"

"One must have a little snack of something special, now and then," Marko said, and they all laughed.

"Look. I know you've got a little pot in your bags. Don't let these people know it, Okay?"

"I didn't bring anything. Did you, Len?"

"No. I know better than to try to get on a plane with anything like that. I'm the type who they strip search on general principles, or something, it sometimes seems. I'm surprised we weren't searched coming here."

"You were with a Ponti. They don't do that with us."

Lenny didn't say anything. The pilot grinned, and said, "No shit? You're a Ponti? And they let you come here?"

"I'm not like a lot of the family. I'm not into their way of doing business. On the other hand, it can save a lot of time and trouble for people to think I am. Sometimes.

"I was in communication with the Howards for months before they asked me to come here. They know who Pops is, but they also know I'm not cast in his mold."

"I met Paulo Ponti, once. I took him to Nassau. He seemed alright, to me, but you can't tell anything about a person from something like that."

"Uncle Paulo is sort of between me and Pops in a lot of our ideas. Pops is like Grampops, a lot. Paulo is more like Grammoms, in psychology. Do your business quietly, and you stay out of all those conflicts. I'm of the psychology that says to get out of the business, altogether. We've already got fifty times what we could ever give away if we spent eighteen hours a day, seven days a week, throwing it out of the car window.

"No one is here to take us to the house?"

"Minute!" He got on the radio, and called. The one who answered said he didn't want to come out there just to give them the keys. They were in the car, the red Porsche, in front of the radio building. There was a map on the seat. Couldn't miss it.

"They leave a new Porsche sitting out there with the house keys on the seat?" Marko asked, unbelieving. The pilot laughed.

"It's an island. What would anyone do with it? The house keys will work if you have the pass code, or something, so they aren't any good to anyone else.

"Got to get back! Call if you need anything! Ciao!" He went back into the plane, and waved, taxied around, and headed down the runway. Marko and Lenny headed for the Porsche. Marko was looking confused and nervous.

"Que paso?" Lenny asked.

"That bit about a pass code. I don't have a clue what it might be."

They got the car, loaded their bags, and headed down the lone road from the airport. The map showed that they would go to the crossroad in the little town and turn right, then follow that road to the south end of the island. It was the place at the end where the road curved around to come back to the other side of the island. There was a note that said to have his passport number ready for if they were stopped, and to call them on the cell phone if they needed anything else. They had his number on the caller ID, so would answer.

"I know the code. It's my passport number. There are no police here to stop anyone. I don't know what that is about the phone. It's only good for calling in the states."

"Maybe there are two codes. Extra security."

It was only four miles to the end of the island. The house was a mansion, sitting on a hilltop, with a lawn more than six hundred feet deep that went to the sparkling water's edge. They could just see it past the house as Marko punched his passport number into the security box. The steel gate silently slid open, he drove in, and the gates as silently closed.

"You know something?" Lenny asked. "This ain't at all bad!"

"So? I'm going to argue the point?"

They went to the massive carved mahogany front entrance. Marko found the key that would open the door, inserted it, turned it – and nothing happened, except a quiet feminine voice said, "What is your entrance code, please?"

"Er ... six five five four five seven four six."

The door opened. "We know what that was there for, don't we?" Lenny asked, with a grin.

They stepped inside, and stood in awe at the open view of a waterfall dropping into a kidney-shaped pool with a lot of colorful fishes and multi-colored water lilies. The inlaid tile floor led to either side of the pool and into doors on either side of a hallway. The hallway ended at a large lanai-type of room with hundreds of hybrid orchids planted on driftwood and in beds under the wood. They were all colors, shapes, and sizes. It looked like a fantasy booth he'd seen at the world orchid show in Miami with Elena, a girl whose mother raised orchids. The sparkling sea was six hundred feet past a lawn that was perfectly maintained. There were two gazebos down by the water's edge, and a wharf with a large boat moored to it. There was a greenhouse to the west, undoubtedly where the plants in the lanai were housed when not in season, or something. There was another house, much smaller, through a garden toward the east. It would be a nice upscale cottage, in the states.

"I think I could get used to living like this – if I really applied myself," Lenny remarked. Marko laughed.

A beautiful dark girl with shiny black hair to below her waist came from the cottage, saw them there, and waved.

"Everywhere you look, it gets better!" Lenny cried.

A boy of two or three years came from the house, and she picked him up and pointed to them. He waved when she told him to. A semi-nude man who looked like a carved mahogany statue of a Greek god came to ask something of her. He turned and waved, then came toward the house with the woman and child.

"I think we've invaded Olympus!" Marko cried.

They were Sandi and Leon Manitos and their son, Martin. They were the staff, and had been with the Howards when they moved there, just over three years and a few months ago. They used to live in Martinique, but things weren't so good there, anymore. Sandi would take care of the house, and he would be around for anything they needed outside. Four local people came from the village every Saturday to do the major regular housework.

They waved, and went back toward their cozy cottage. Marko was staring at Leon with a strange look on his face.

"What's the matter?" Lenny asked.

"I've never been turned on by a guy before," Marko answered. "I think, if he said to drop my drawers and bend over, I would!"

Lenny looked at the trio, and grinned.

"You know something? I haven't either! What a rush!

"I do have one question, though."

"What's that?"

"What in hell are we doing here, housesitting a house with a live-in staff?"

Marko considered. "I don't know, but I *ain't* gonna object!"

Sandi came to show them their rooms, and to ask if they wanted her to cook up something. They could have almost anything they wanted. The freezer was fully stocked. If they wanted to take the boat or anything, just push the call button on the door to the gear house on the dock, and Leon would come.

Lenny's room was connected to Marko's through a shared all-marble bath with gold-plated fixtures. There was a large TV, hooked to a satellite dish, and a desktop computer in each room. There was a large bar on the end of the beachside lanai that had anything Lenny ever heard of in stock. He didn't know from wines, but there was a whole basement-like room full of very obviously fine old wines. He knew the Rothschild labels were supposed to be worth more than he made a year per bottle.

They decided they would just cook up something they found in the kitchen for tonight, and would decide what to do about their meals tomorrow. The "little" freezer in the kitchen had a lot of things, and Lenny had once been a cook in a fancy restaurant. He knew how to cook some special dishes, and he did like to cook. He found various seafoods in reasonably small containers, and made a sort of paella. He was going to fake the saffron, but found a fairly large sealed jar of the real thing. It had to contain three hundred dollars worth of pure saffron!

It was going to be far too much for two people. He said, "What the hell?" and called Sandi to invite her and Leon for dinner. She paused, then accepted. When they came in, she said, "I had to come! The guest invites the cook to dinner!"

Leon, who was in nothing but a bathing suit, asked if he should dress.

"What for? The food tastes the same if you're dressed or nude," Lenny said. "Sit! We'll start with some of this wine. I don't know much about wine, so I took the first clear red I saw.

"Marko? If you will pour?"

Marko dropped a white towel across his forearm, stuck his nose in the air, and sniffed as he applied the corkscrew and popped the cork. He let the wine sit a moment while he brought wine glasses, then poured a bit across the cork into Leon's glass and offered the cork to him. He shrugged.

"You sniff the cork to see that the wine's not sour or anything," Sandi instructed. He smelled the cork, and said it smelled alright to him.

"Now you take a small sip from the glass, and swirl it around in your mouth, then say it is good or to throw it out and bring something decent."

He took a small taste, and said, "That's damned good! I usually don't care for wine!"

"Not to form, but it'll do!" Marko said, and poured them all a glass. He poured a little dribble in Martin's glass, and filled it with water. "We do that in Italy, where I only was once for less than two weeks."

They chatted for a few minutes, and became friends. Lenny brought in the paella, and Marko served it. It had come out perfect, but paella was always as good as the ingredients – and these were the best to be had. They debated whether to go into the village that night, but soon decided they were too tired, and the village would still be there tomorrow. They went to bed. Lenny was still puzzled about why they were there, at all, but wasn't about to bring it up again.

The morning was beautiful. It was more colorful than any sunset Lenny had ever seen, golds and pinks and salmons and a little red. He was always up before dawn, before anyone else. He made a pot of good special Panamanian coffee and went out on the lanai to see Leon and Sandi coming toward the house. They waved, and Leon went on around front, while Sandi came in to make breakfast for them. He said he didn't eat much for breakfast, but she insisted she had to cook something to prove she could, after last night. She would make an omelet.

"I call it pizza omelet. It tastes like a cheese and mushroom pizza!"

Marko came out about half an hour later, carrying a cup of the coffee. Sandi brought out her omelets, which sent Marko into a state of ecstasy. Pizza was his favorite food, and this tasted like the best mushroom pizza he ever had!

They decided they would take the boat out to cruise all the way around the island to see what there was to see. Leon came around, and checked the boat out, saying it was in good shape and ready. He could pilot it or they could go alone, whatever they preferred.

Lenny didn't know anything about boats, and Marko had almost no experience. Maybe Leon could teach him about handling it. They invited Sandi along, but she had her duties, and had seen the island from the water a hundred times, already.

They went around the island to the village on the northern end, and went to the docks there to walk around the place. There was one bar and one restaurant that catered to the locals, though the people on the island would sometimes patronize the places when they were in town. They met the Phillips in the restaurant, having a coconut, banana and pineapple chicha (sort of a blender/juice mix). They seemed very nice people, who were liked by the locals. Leon said they were from the oil family, he believed, or maybe the pharma-ceutical company. They had never met the Howards, directly, so far as he knew, because the Howards stayed mostly at the place, except for Julian. Julian came into town fairly often. He was gay, and the men here made no secret about liking sex, whatever direction it came from.

"And you?" Marko asked.

"It's not really my thing. I have a wife, and am very happy without outside distractions of any type. Who here could compare to Sandi?"

"There's that!" Marko agreed.

They bought some colorful shirts and bathing suits of the bikini type that were popular there. Leon said that the food and lifestyle on the island meant people didn't get fat. Fat people looked ridiculous in tighter clothes. Lenny couldn't help noticing that the people here were all very healthy and handsome. He hadn't seen anyone not in top physical shape. He was beginning to feel insecure about it, but knew a few days of exercise would tone him up. Neither he nor Marko were in shape, but they both had good physical structure.

"I see the people here aren't the piggy type. I haven't seen anybody very skinny, and no one is fat," he remarked.

"Our food isn't full of things that make it taste good, but hurts your health. It's natural," Leon pointed out.

"It tastes natural," Lenny agreed. "It's filling, so you don't keep stuffing your face."

"Yeah. MSG," Marko replied, sourly. "Pops has a company that makes the crap by the ton, but we can't have it in the house. That's the kind of thing I hate about what he considers business."

"What do you mean?" Lenny asked.

"MSG. It's in everything, almost anywhere, anymore."

"But ... I know some people are allergic. I am, a little. What else? It really makes food taste good."

Leon laughed. "It makes you hungry. Your body has all the food you need, but you keep eating. Your mind translates the hungry part as good flavor. Wine does that, just a little, but not so extreme."

"Makes you hungry? I still don't get it!"

"Ah, Pops said he figured that out in nineteen fifty," Marko replied. "He used to go to a Chinese restaurant in New York for the best tasting food ever, but he would eat a big meal and be starving an hour later. They had always used MSG. Pops tasted a little directly, and said it didn't have any taste, to him – then got hungry, fifteen minutes later, after he'd had a steak and potato meal!

"He did some tests. He put some in one of his meals one night, and was starving, an hour later. He had the same meal the next night without it, and didn't get hungry until breakfast. He did it with several things, and it was always the same. He figured it was a goldmine, because he studied it and could make a ton of it for about four dollars. He packaged it and sold it as a flavor enhancer. It went from a little thing in the supermarkets in a little part of Queens to a national product in less than a year. All those testimonials about how everything Mary cooked was so blah, then she used it, and now everyone raved about her cooking, and couldn't get enough! There was never a leftover scrap anymore! It was the same food as always, but Googledebump made it *s-o-o-o-o-o* special!

"Off the soapbox. I'm almost ashamed when I go to the store and that shit's on the shelf for hundreds of lardtubs to contaminate their meals with."

Leon laughed again. "We figured that out when I was about four. Mother got some packaged macaroni and cheese dinner that we all went ape over. She said it was so expensive, and she could make the same thing. A little mild cheddar and macaroni. We ate hers, but it was, like you said, blah. She couldn't figure it, so read the label, in case there was some spice or something they used. It was the same thing, except it had MSG. She bought some and tried it. It worked, so she put it in other food. We all ate like horses, and started to get fat, so she cut it out, and we never had it again. We all went right back to our normal weight.

"The people here know what the stuff is. They were so strong about it that the town council here outlawed it. Just go to St. Elvan's or any other close island where they sell the stuff and you can see most of the people are much fatter."

"Maybe that's why I'm not fat," Lenny said. "I'm mildly allergic. It gives me pretty violent headaches, so I've always avoided anything that has it. I have to admit that most restaurants use it, anymore. I can't eat in most of them. Gregor's and Boli's have no MSG on the menu, so I eat there when I eat out.

"Those Chinese noodle things I have sometimes have it. I learned to not use the flavor packs, just some catsup, or whatever."

"Read the damned ingredients in those flavor packs. They're listed as to which is most used. MSG is always first. If it was a true flavor enhancer, it would be way down where salt is," Marko said. "I won't worry about that here, for sure!

"Well! Let's go back to the house. I can handle the boat, now, so we can go out anytime we like. Leon probably doesn't care to babysit a couple of twenty year old kids."

They went back around the lush island to the point. The house was a magnificent sight on the hill on the end of the island. It's design seemed to flow into the hill like a natural feature. That it was hugely expensive was obvious, but in an understated way. It was not ostentatious.

They explored the entire place and the end of the island, that day. In the hottest part, between about noon and three o'clock, they stayed in the house. Lenny used the computer to e-mail people and to brag about the place. He found a digital camera in the secretary desk, and took hundreds of pictures, edited for the best, and sent them to friends. He received a few e-mails he answered, then went onto the lanai to lay in a hammock to watch the few boats coming and going out to sea.

His mind went back to the question he had asked last night. With that staff living here, what were they there for? All expenses paid? Fancy cars and boats? Freezers full of gourmet foods? A wine cellar with at least a million dollars worth of the best wines to be had? Gold-plated bathroom fixtures?

He wasn't about to complain! He couldn't help but worry that something wasn't right, here in this paradise. He suspected that what wasn't right was his being there. What was it he didn't know?

The lunch Sandi prepared had lots of fresh vegetables. He supposed they were grown on the island, but hadn't seen evidence of it, except for little vegetable patches by the native houses.

There was a large breadfruit tree by the end of the house. He never cared much for it, always saying it tasted like library paste, but Sandi had some French-fried at lunch. She had a hint of garlic in it. It was delicious. There were many pineapples, bananas, coconuts, guavas, and dozens of fruits he'd never heard of growing all over the island. He would soon know many of them, and like them.

They spent more than an hour swimming in the pristine crystal water. Lenny said he was going to get back into a presentable shape. The natives made him feel like a lazy sloth. He swam until he was almost exhausted, then laid in the hammock awhile, then swam a few minutes more, then rinsed, and they went into a delicious curry for dinner. Marko insisted that they all eat together at lunch, with which Lenny fully agreed.

They decided to let things happen at the spur of the moment, to the greatest degree. A lot of questions would be answered, in time – such as: why were he and Marko here in this paradise?

They went into the town, just after dark. and to the little bar. Marko said that was a bust when they walked in, because the only female there was the barmaid. There were about fifteen men. The people were very friendly there, and they had a good time. They weren't competing with anyone for anything, and there were a lot of stories about the sea and whatever came up. They relaxed. The night most definitely was *not* a bust!

When the beautiful girl (whose husband owned the bar. Damn!) came to say last call, Lenny was surprised to see it was midnight. Time had passed so pleasantly he'd lost track.

He drove, going back. Marko wouldn't drive if he'd had more than one beer. Lenny didn't really have many, and wasn't feeling at all drunk. He was extra careful, and drove a bit more slowly than usual, but it was an easy drive, and they got to bed before one.

Lenny wondered if, just maybe, this lifestyle would become boring very quickly. He looked around to see the moonlight dancing on the waves, and decided, no. He could look at that, the sea, the moonlight, the people, the food ... there were hundreds of things to do. He wouldn't become bored for more than a few hours, at most.

He turned in. He was still up before dawn, as usual. He was well-rested, and feeling good, so he did a few exercises, then went to watch the spectacular sunrise. Sandi came to the house, and said she was going to fix something else for breakfast. Cinnamon pancakes. She saw the pot of coffee brewing, and grinned.

Marko came out just after the sunrise, and said this place was really good for him. He usually had trouble waking himself up before nine, and here it was a quarter to seven, and he was awake and ready to tackle the world!

Sandi brought out the pancakes. There was nothing except butter to put on them, then Lenny remembered they were cinnamon pancakes, so probably didn't need jelly.

He tasted one. It was a cinnamon flavor, with a slight trace of coconut and walnut. They were delicious! She said the walnut was artificial, they didn't have them there, but everything else was natural.

Lenny and Marko decided to go fishing. They heard stories last night about the tuna running, so they would see if they could catch one. Marko had been deepsea fishing with his family off of Miami, and knew generally how to go about it. Leon said to go south, about four kilometers, then move slowly westward. The tuna followed a current there. Be sure the tackle was secured, because there were some very big bluefins, this time of year.

They went out and followed the instructions. Lenny was glad he'd secured the heavy rod, because it was jerked out of his hands after only a few minutes of fishing. It slammed to the end of its tether and hung suspended there. It took both of them to drag it back to where it could be put back into the sling/holder.

Marko had one, too. It wasn't as big, and the rod hadn't been jerked out of the sling/holder. He stopped the engine, and they fought their fish. Marko brought his to the side of the boat, after about ten minutes. It was about 80 pounds. Lenny was suddenly worried that he might have a big shark or something, because he'd made no progress in bringing his alongside.

It was more than forty minutes later when he got his first glimpse of his prize. It was tiring (like he *wasn't?*) and he was able to bring it to about thirty feet away, when it came to the surface. Marko cried, "Shit! You've caught Moby Dick!"

Twenty minutes later, it was alongside. It took both of them and the winch to drag it over into the boat. It took up most of the room in the boat.

"How ... what test is that line? That damned thing has to weight half a ton!" Marko exclaimed.

Lenny was laying prone on the deck, totally exhausted. He had the shakes, and was too weak to move.

They had drifted a long way. They couldn't see any islands, or anything else. Marko radioed to Leon, who told him to set the autopilot to a GPS number. There was nothing between to hit, so it would take them back. When they were about half a kilometer off the island, turn off the autopilot.

"What's the test of the line we're using?" Marko asked.

"Got one that broke it? It's five hundred pound test."

"No, we got the thing aboard, but I thought it would weigh a lot more than any five hundred pounds. We're bringing it in. I caught one that weights about eighty pounds, but this is a whale!"

Leon laughed, and said he'd have a couple of the men from the village there to help them clean it. They could get pictures. Would it be alright to tell the villagers they could have some of it?

"We'll keep Marko's, and they can have mine. I doubt we have room in the freezer for ten percent of it!"

"They will appreciate it. I'll tell them to bring ice chests for ... what would you estimate it weighs?"

"It's seven feet long."

"Four hundred or a bit more. Ever caught anything bigger?"

"The biggest fish I ever caught before was a two and a half pound trout!" Lenny said, from his position on the deck. "I fought it three minutes! I fought this one about fifty hours, the way I feel!"

"Been sick yet?"

"I feel a little queasy, but mostly just too tired to get up. I'm laying on the deck."

"When the boat starts moving, you're going to be sick. Get to the rail, and hang over, when you start back. Believe me, you're going to be very glad you did that!"

They chatted a half minute more, nd Marko set the autopilot and started the engine. Lenny just made the rail when the boat started. He vomited more than he thought possible, ending with stomach-wrenching dry heaves. Marko said it was too much adrenalin for too long. He gave him a glass of water with ground ginger in it. He didn't want to chance it, but drank. There were a couple of sharp thrusts by his stomach, then it stopped. He as much as passed out on the deck. The last thing he heard was Marko saying, "I'll be damned! It works!"

Lenny came to in the cabin, on a mat. There were several men on the dock, cleaning his fish and telling jokes. There were three pretty women packing the huge thick steaks into ice chests. There was an ice machine in the gear house on the dock that Leon had opened for them. Lenny staggered to the dock, and they made good-natured fun of him. Leon said to look in a full-length mirror! Fighting that fish did more than what twenty hours of swimming could do to his body!

He gave him the finger, and went to look in the mirror at the end of the cabin. It was true. His pecs and biceps were larger and smoother toned, and he had sixpack abs for the first time in five years!

"That's mostly dehydration," Leon cautioned. "You probably did burn off some fat layer. You should drink about two quarts of water for the rest of the afternoon.

"Sandi has your lunch ready. It's late, but you should be hungry after that."

He was. He went inside, where Marko was just finishing his lunch. "Yankee pot roast!" he said. "I used to love it. She does it better than Aunt Sara, and she did it great!

"How you feeling?"

"Surprisingly, very good!"

"You really look good. Like you've just spent ten days at the gym. We both can use a bit more exercise."

They chatted a bit, while Lenny ate. He said he was definitely going to get fat if he kept eating like that. Sandi said she didn't use fat in the cooking, just the natural flavors of the meat and vegetables. Always eat a big meal in the middle of the day, so you can burn it off before dinner, then have a cool and light dinner, and limit the beers. Two beers were fine. Three were too many. Drink wine, instead. Sad as it was, vodka wouldn't make you fat, but rum could, if it was too sweet.

A small very fast boat came to the dock. Sandi looked out, and said it was Julian. She didn't know he would be back so soon, but they would find he was good company. Everyone on the island liked him, some more than others (with a wink).

"Ha! Do you worry about Leon around him?" Marko asked.

She laughed. "I didn't know if you knew, so I did that to make you ask why, if you didn't. I don't think Leon is interested in that kind of thing, and he's married, so I don't worry. Julian is clean and safe and careful, so I don't think I would worry if they were together, so long as it wasn't too much."

"How refreshingly rare!" Lenny cried. "A woman who knows she has nothing to worry about, which I could figure from being around you. Leon could turn on a statue, I think. I actually wondered what I'd do if he suggested anything."

"He won't suggest anything, but most of the men here would like for him to suggest something, I think. He is a wonderful man. He's so handsome, and such a good soul."

Julian had come onto the dock, and was hugging everybody there. He was handsome, himself, tannish, blond, and athletic build. He was about five ten, the same as Lenny. He was obviously popular. With the women, as well as with the men.

After a few minutes on the dock, he heaved a large maleta from the boat, and headed for the house. Sandi called to him as he came into the lanai, and he went to hug her and to play for a minute with Martin, who came running from inside the house when he came onto the lanai. Sandi introduced them, and said they were guests from the states. He frankly sized them up, and shook hands, saying they would be somebody new to talk with, and go fishing, or whatever. Leon told him that Lenny caught the tuna they were cleaning on the dock, and that they had already cleaned one Marko caught, and had it in the freezer.

"Most people in the states don't know how good tuna steaks are. They think tuna is only from cans."

They chatted for a few minutes. They liked Julian ("Call me Juli"). He was very open and intelligent, and didn't put a false face on anything.

"We'll go into town tonight. I'll introduce you to some people," Juli promised. "As for now, I need a long shower and some rest." He waved, and went to his rooms. Lenny and Marko went down to the dock, where the people were just finishing working with the tuna. They chatted with the people until they all took their ice chests, loaded them into the truck, and left – except for a young man called Samuel, who went to the house. Leon grinned. They returned the grin.

It was the hot part of the day, so Lenny and Marko went to the house, Marko to lay in a hammock on the lanai, and Lenny to use the internet. At about four thirty, Lenny went down to the ocean and swam for half an hour, very much liking the way his body seemed to be thanking him for the exercise. Marko came down a bit later, and went swimming. Leon, Sandi, and Martin came to swim, stripping off before going into the water. Sandi was as spectacular and unselfconscious nude as when clothed. Martin was a good swimmer, at two years of age. Sandi explained that anyone who lived surrounded by deep water who didn't teach their children to swim as soon as they taught them to walk was a fool.

After awhile, they all showered and put on their clothes, those who had stripped. Lenny wondered why

Leon stripped, when he was living in a bathing suit, anyhow. They went to the house. Lenny and Marko shaved and such before dinner. Samuel and Juli came from his rooms to dinner with them. Everyone seemed comfortable with everyone else. It was a pleasant meal of fingers of tuna and of a potato-like vegetable Sandi said was yuca, and a multi-fruit/ vegetable salad with a mayonnaise-based dressing that was delicious. They finished the meal, and got in the Porsche to go into town. They went to the bar there, where Lenny and Marko met several of the people from the states. They seemed to be very regular types. They were introduced to several natives they hadn't met the night before. It seemed nobody could get enough opportunity to hug Juli, some holding on for a lot longer than would seem necessary. Marko and Lenny grinned at Lou and Marcia Stevens, who they were sharing a table with. Lou said they would have to get used to the way people were here. It was a lot different than the states, on some things.

About eleven, the Pages, Arthur and Evelynne, came in. Lenny felt the mood of the bar change when they walked into the door, and wondered about it. They didn't seem to notice.

"A couple of our pains-in-the-ass gringos," Lou said. "They're pretentive, and don't even know that these people don't like them. They think the people treat everyone the way they treat them. That ass even had the temerity to tell me he thought it was just a burden *we* have to share that they resent *us* for having so much. I told him I hadn't noticed anything wrong with the way they treated me.

He said it wasn't wrong. "They can't help it if they're jealous. It's the way they were raised."

Marcia added, "I said we all have to live with the way we were raised. It went ten miles over his head."

"There are only five people here who don't fit. You can bet Jim Hedges will be in, if they are. They like to sit around and talk about how primitive and savage these people are, and how much better things are somewhere else," Lou said. "They think other gringos are jealous of them because of what they have. I doubt there are ten people who don't have a lot more than they do. We don't talk about money, they don't talk about much else. That alone shows who's the have and who's the have-not.

"Sorry. That type get me to ranting."

"We'd better go before Hedges gets here," Marcia suggested. "You know how you always want to, as you say, smack the obsequious asshole son of a bitch in the puss."

They said they had enjoyed the conversation, but she was right. No sense in letting such a pleasant evening be ruined, when all they had to do was leave half an hour earlier than usual.

They said their goodnights to everyone, and went out. They weren't out the door when the Pages came over to introduce themselves. "I'm Art Page, and this is Evelynne, my better half. We see you're new here. Guests of someone?"

"Leonard and Marcus," Lenny replied, not mentioning a last name. "We're guests of the Howards. We came with Juli to get a taste of the place. He's so popular we get swamped when we're at the same table, as you can see. We're circulating and meeting people."

"Well, there are some worth the trouble. You were talking to the Stevens when we came in," Evelynne said.

"They're of good family, but seem a bit stiff, if you know what I mean. Julian is a bit of a problem for the Howards, I would think. They send him out here to keep him and his ... lifestyle, if you will ... away from the higher society, or so I've heard. It must be terribly embarrassing to them."

"Really?" Marko asked. "They didn't seem that way to me. They introduced us and said we would have a very good time here, because he knows everyone, and everyone likes him. So far, that's been the way it goes. There doesn't seem to be much of the stupid snobbery here that we have in the states."

"Well, we're in a position where we have a lot of people who resent us because we have so much, and they don't have anything," Marcia said, condescendingly. "Arthur owns a lot of large businesses, particularly banking interests, so he has a particularly large portion of resentful people to contend with. You probably don't understand what it means to the common types to be faced with someone who has made so much."

"Money? Your father is one of the richest men in the whole country, isn't he, Marcus? I've never heard him speak of money, but people in that level don't. Ever. We consider it declasse.

"Oh! Would you like another beer? Arthur? Evelynne?"

"Er, we don't drink *beer*!" Arthur said. "I wish they had a decent wine here, but that's too much to dream of. I'll have a Chivas Regal on the rocks. I know they have that. Evelynne will have a Tanqueray and tonic with a twist."

"Chivas? Oh, well. Okay," Marko replied, waved for the waitress, and gave her the order. Two beers and the drinks.

"Er, you don't care for Chivas Regal? It's a fine scotch."

"Oh, I only like Haig Scots Whiskey," Marko said, with a wave. "I'm not much for whiskeys."

"Haig and Haig? It's alright, I guess," Arthur countered. "On the order of those Walker things."

"No. Haig. It's rare, so I suppose you might not have come across it."

Arthur and Evelynne looked totally confused. He wanted to say something, but didn't.

"What business is your father into?" Evelynne asked, to change the subject.

"What business *isn't* he into would be easier to answer!" Lenny said, with a laugh.

"Please! Let's not talk shop after business hours," Marko said. "It's to get away from that crap that we're here."

The girl brought the drinks, and a sour-looking bullish man came in to look around, then came to the table. He announced, "Jim Hedges. Oil, steel, brokerage, insurance, commercial development, and all that."

"Marcus and Leonard, layabouts and bums," Marko said. "He's Lenny."

"I don't think a bum or layabout would be here on this island. It's rather exclusive. What are you really into?"

"We're mostly into not talking about money or business when we're on vacation," Lenny replied. "As you just noted, we wouldn't be here if we weren't a notch above that.

"We really got some great fish today. Toward the southeast. Tuna."

"They're guests of the Howards. They came in with *Julian*," Marcia said.

"The island's fruit? Er, I mean, if you ... it's a joke. I've never met the Howards. I don't know much about them, or what business they're in."

Lenny felt evil. "I'm not sure. I know they have a few million ounces of gold and more silver and not a small cache of platinum in several banks. It was on their computer when I used it, I warned them not to leave that kind of information laying around like that."

"Er? Millions of ounces? Of gold?" Hedges cried, eyes wide.

"Well, that was just the Mexico City thing. They have a lot more in other places."

"They should like today!" Evelynne gushed. "Gold went to over a thousand five hundred dollars an ounce, in some markets!"

"Why would they even care?" Marko asked, innocently. "Pops has a lot of gold, and he doesn't give a damn about the market today or tomorrow. No matter what happens to the market, gold retains its value. If it's worth a lot, the market's down, and money isn't worth a lot. Big deal.

"I thought we weren't going to talk about anything as crass as money."

"Well, money is very important in today's world!" Evelynne cried. "It's security in an insecure world!"

"Tell that to the people who had billions in the land market a few years ago. Billionaires tonight, flat broke in the morning," Marko said. "If you'll excuse us, we'll want to circulate and meet some of these people."

"Why would you want to meet *them*?" Hedges demanded.

"They're good people with a realistic sense of values," Lenny answered, as he and Marko got up and went over to Juli's table. Hedges and the Pages were looking shocked.

"Met the pill-pusses, eh?" Juli asked, with a grin.

"What a thrill!" Marko fired back.

"We're going to a friend's place. Want to come along? It's not much different than here, but that type does *not* go there."

"I'll take a rain check on it," Lenny replied. "Marko can do as he pleases."

"You're not together?" he asked, surprised.

"Together?"

"Like Samuel and I, only steady."

"No. We're not gay, but Leon makes you stop and wonder."

"God! He's a god! He drives me crazy!" he wailed. "So. You're available to teach a new lifestyle to?"

They laughed. "I'm not without experience. It's just not my thing," he said. Marko said, "Ditto. It's not bad, but it's not my thing, either."

"Well, you might not like my friend's place – but you might."

"We'll take the rain check. We're looking for new experiences," Marko said, with a grin. "Can we get a cab back, or something?"

"Take the car. I'll probably not go back tonight, so I'll see you in the morning."

In the morning, Lenny decided to go for a swim early, then returned to the house, where Sandi had breakfast cooking. Fish cakes, this morning. They were as good as everything she fixed.

Marko wandered in about seven thirty. They discussed what they would do today. Lenny was all for exploring the island, itself. He would walk into town on the east side, and back on the west. He always liked walking, and would learn a lot more that way than from a car. He could walk the entire circle before noon, but would take a lot longer. He would carry the camera, and take a lot of pictures. He could stay in the town for the hot part of the day, and walk back in the afternoon. Marko would spend the day around the place, and maybe take a jetski to explore along the coastline.

He started walking, and stopped at a couple of places, whenever there was someone outside to introduce himself to. Everyone he met seemed more than ordinarily nice. He explained about staying at the Howard's place, and they all said it was a very nice place to stay. Only one had ever been there when their son had been there from Germany, and had met and become friends with Julian. He didn't ask anything more about that, but wondered what the deal was, there. Mrs. Marks, with whom he was speaking, noted the pause, and said that they knew Julian was gay. They didn't ask questions about their son, but he had since married the girl he was living with in Germany, so probably not. Ideas were different here than in Europe or the US. The

Howards were fine people, and Julian was a very good person, and that's all that counts.

After about an hour, a couple of natives came to walk with him. He had met one, Silvio, at the bar the first night. Benito, the other, had seen him last night at the bar, but hadn't been introduced. They were both close friends with Juli.

It was an altogether pleasant walk, until around ten thirty. Benito and Silvio had turned in at a place where they were the caretakers. It was a lot like the Howard's place.

The next house, he had been semi-warned about stopping. They said the person there was not popular. You may have seen him last evening at the bar. Hedges.

His luck must be turning sour. Hedges was out on the road in front of his place. He said he was policing the area for garbage the trash that lived there, the natives, that is, threw out of their cars.

Lenny had seen one car and one truck that was the property of natives. He didn't mention that there weren't any cars for the crap to be thrown out of. The sack Hedges carried contained one small scrap of paper, and a soda can. He was making it sound like the natives were using his place for their collective garbage dump.

"Come on in. I'll fix some tea, or something."

He was about to refuse, but maybe he could learn something from talking to the ass. They went inside to a huge room with a glass wall toward the ocean. It was angled to the northeast to avoid the sun shining through half the day. The view was very good, if not quite as spectacular as the Howards' place.

Hedges fixed some iced tea (that he'd boiled, turning it sour) and sat at the marble-topped table. They chatted about fish and such for a few minutes, then, "Leonard, I've never met the Howards for more than a 'Hello' at the market, or such. They're fairly new here. Julian is much talked about because he's gay, but that doesn't bother me. I went through a stage in my teens where I ... whatever. He seems popular with the people here, and I have to admit that the men are all unusually handsome, and seem to like the ... relationships.

"Where I grew up, a hundred miles from Topeka, Kansas, they wouldn't even admit there was such a thing. We were made to feel guilty about even letting another boy see you nude. When you get to the stage at thirteen or fourteen where you fool around, and even screw each other at the swimming pond, you hide it. You know for a fact that almost everyone did those things, you just didn't admit it.

"Larry, my best friend, and I hid in the willow trees by the pond and watched almost everyone we knew our age doing the same things. We saw this one old, well, he was maybe thirty five, but that was old to us, guy blowing Sam and Bruce when they were fourteen and fifteen. We got excited by it, and jerked each other off. We ended up screwing each other a couple of days later, when they did it again.

"Anyhow, I just want to say that I don't think anything about Julian and all the men here. I get a little turned on by some of them, myself, to be honest. They're so innocent about it, and you can tell they respect each other.

"I don't know how to ask another man if he's gay or if he likes being with a gay."

"No. Marko isn't either. Julian thought we were together, that way. He asked, and I answered the same way. It doesn't bother me that anyone here asks, though I'd probably get upset if they did, in the states. Different cultural aspect.

"I don't really know. I had the same type of experiences you did, to a point, but don't really remember particularly liking it. I liked getting off, and that's all it was about. No emotional content.

"I think there's a lot of emotional content with Juli and his friends. They really care about each other. That was the part that keeps you turned off, in the states. You would never admit to liking another man to nearly the point you liked getting fucked. Here, I don't know. I might. I can't believe how I reacted to Leon."

"I think that one's about the handsomest man I ever saw. He's built to put the statue of David to shame. His wife would put Venus to shame," he replied. "I think I would like very much to get fucked by him. I don't know if he'd be interested in that, though."

"No. I asked him. He says having someone like Sandi was more than anyone could ask in life. He doesn't want anyone else.

"What's this about?"

"I'm ... I know I made a bad impression on you and your friend last night. I know I do that with the natives, and some of the gringos. It's because I came here all money and possessions and no family and no real friends. I came here thinking I had more than ninety five percent of the world, and I was going to enjoy it to the hilt!

"I met the man who built this place for me. He's married, and has three kids, and he seduced me. I think I'd never enjoyed sex more in my life, he seemed to think it was fun, and we understood each other better because he fucked me.

"I always figured that you got all the women you wanted if you had money, but the ones here make it damned plain that they aren't interested.

"That's when I turned from a sort of obnoxious ass into a total shithead. I've been scared that I'm queer, and didn't know it. I held myself away from it by becoming what I come across as now. It was getting better, and I went to some of the nearer places to meet women. I want a family. I'm a different person when I'm not here.

"It was working out. I was leveling off and convincing myself that I didn't do anything out of the ordinary anymore than when I was fourteen. I didn't really consider that kind of life, actually.

"Then the Howards came, and Julian, this really handsome gay man was always around, and was always hugging the guys, and they were all plainly wanting him. I met Leon, and wanted nothing more in life than for him to screw me until my eyeballs rolled up in their sockets.

"Then I saw everyone looked at him very much like I did. Julian was doing nothing more than being honest about his feelings and what he wanted. Do you know that he sometimes goes with women? They all claim he's the greatest lover since Don Juan!

"The truth? I don't know what this is about. I just had to see what would happen if I was honest with someone."

"Nothing. Most people have been there, done that. They grew up where it wasn't so extreme as Topeka. We're not in Kansas anymore, Toto! I'm from the east, and the way it's talked about is the same, to an extent, but we every damned one know it's all talk, that we've done the same things."

"Should I get married, or try to emulate Julian?"

"Why the hell ask me?! If you really want a family, and can really care for the mother, go for it. If you can't, go for the other way. I can only say that you'll never be where Juli is. It's not a natural part of you that you can accept as being natural."

"Which is why I'd already decided the only way to live is to get out of here and to a place where paradise isn't inverted. It always will be to me, here. Why live in paradise if you can't enjoy it?"

"That's a good way to put it. Inverted paradise.

"Would it still be paradise if it was inverted?"

Hedges grinned. "I suppose, but not for you or me. If you're like Julian, it would be."

"I wonder if ... the norm here is bisexual. I think it is paradise for Julian, and for the natives. It's still paradise for almost everybody else, but not in the same way. The Pages are strictly hetero. It can never be paradise for them. I doubt they can ever find paradise, no matter where or what. They can't let go of their upbringing, which is why they don't have a tiny clue as to why people treat them the way they do."

"They don't even know they're treated any differently. Paradise has to come from inside, and it's not there. There's no place for it there. I deny it, because I resist it. You're right. It was my psychological upbringing. The people here don't have the stupid taboos, and are happy.

"Be honest. Have you seen any sign whatever that a native here isn't happy? I wonder if you can have that. I doubt it. I know I can't"

Lenny thought for a minute, then nodded slowly. He considered things as possibilities and "What ifs?" He wasn't really considering that things might actually happen.

He soon said he'd better go. Hedges said he would drive into town later to put his place on the market. The people would be glad to see him go. He now understood, he'd come to the conclusion before this conversation, that the people didn't hate him like he'd thought. They pitied him.

With cause.

Lenny was in the town just after noon, so he went into the restaurant for a good meal. He greeted and was greeted by most of the people there. The meal of the day was a lobster chowder that was superb.

It was the hot part of the day. He decided to wait there in town for the cooler part, so sat with a peach nectar drink at the little table to the side of the market. People would come and go. He talked to several. He got an offer to spend the time with a man his age he'd talked with twice in the bar whose wife was visiting her parents on St. Elvan's. They'd hit it off very well, and Jon was truly interesting and was as truly interested in him. He was surprised when he found himself honestly considering it, but said he couldn't get into that right now. Jon said he understood, that many people from the states took some time before they decided if it would be right for them. Some, it was. Some, it wasn't. Some would never know.

Lenny thought for a minute. He looked up to meet Jon's eyes, and said, "You're right. Let's go!"

Lenny was more than a little confused. He couldn't deny he'd had as good a time as he ever had, that he'd thrown his inhibitions to the wind, and was damned glad he had. He was confused by what he felt and now was feeling about Jon. He knew he was over-reacting to a situation. He knew he cared for a virtual stranger more than he'd cared for anyone in a very long time. It had come because he got to know Jon very well, very quickly, and he respected him more than he could believe for being a totally honest man.

He was much more surprised because it wasn't the sex. It was the person with whom he shared the sex.

He hadn't shared sex before. He'd had sex. He also remembered his thoughts when Jon was talking with him at the table. He wasn't talking *to* him, he was talking *with* him. There was a real difference, and it was enormous. There was a difference in having sex and sharing sex. It was enormous. It was what Leon and Sandi had – shared. It was what proved that paradise came from inside. As Jon had said, he hadn't come to paradise. He came with paradise to a setting where it fit.

He thought of Hedges' remarks about the Pages. They would never know paradise. They didn't bring anything with them to any setting that would allow it. The people here had it in them, and were in the setting.

Truth be told, Lenny Hamilton was feeling better and far more complete than he ever dreamed he could. If that meant he was gay, he would welcome his inverted paradise.

Could he have this with the other men here? Could he have it with a woman? After all, Jon was very happily married. This took nothing away from that, it added to it.

This was crazy!

It was a good crazy.

Lenny went into the gate and to the house. Marko was out in the ocean on a jetski. Julian had come home, and had brought a girl he thought Marko would like, because they seemed to have the same kind of sense of humor and odd slant on some things. It was, apparently, a good match, because she was out there with him.

"Find any diversion on your tour?" Juli asked.

"Yes. I convinced Hedges he should get the hell out of here and go somewhere he could be accepted – and I got seduced. By a guy."

"Anyone I know?"

"Come on! He lives on this island!"

Juli laughed. "So? Who?"

Jon wouldn't care if he told. "Jon."

"Sexy Jon? He's a dream, in bed! He likes to cuddle and pet. He's a warm person, and a good person."

Lenny nodded. "He's emotionally warm."

Juli considered. "I like that. He's not only a god to look at, he's emotionally warm. That describes him.

"Marko won't go for it. I sort of thought you might. I'm glad it was with Jon, so you'll know how it can be when you get someone not quite the thing you need."

"I suppose that's inevitable. Sooner or later, if you continue it. I probably won't. This was the best sex I have ever had, but that was because of Jon. It might not be possible with anyone else."

"You're wrong. It was because of Jon and *you*. What can happen is based on the combination. It can happen again. You're not in love with Jon, and he's not in love with you, but you do care. If you can communicate, it can happen. It happens a lot, for me."

"You know something? I think you hit it square on the head. Communicate. I was thinking how I didn't talk *to* Jon, I talked *with* Jon. Sandi and Leon don't talk *to* one another, they talk *with*. That's where it comes from."

"That's the first important sign."

"I think maybe I could live the bisexual lifestyle the men do here. It's open and honest. The one thing I'm confused about is whether I'm in love with Jon. I'm wondering about that. I've always said that when a man wonders if he's falling in love, he already has."

"No. I think you might love Jon. I know I do. You're not in love with Jon. He's freed you."

Again, Lenny considered. "I think maybe you've hit it on the head. Again."

They talked for more than an hour. Marko came back with Selene, and headed for town, after a quick shower and shave. Lenny wasn't invited, and didn't expect to be. Juli was taking him to see a friend. He said he definitely didn't want any gang bangs or that kind of thing. Juli said nobody here went for that, to any extent, that it was up to him whether or not anything happened. For most, nothing happened.

Next was a long swim to relax. His body was tightening up faster and better than he thought it would, but he was getting a lot of exercise, and was eating well. He couldn't stop wondering about dozens of things, but decided he would never have answers if he denied the things wherein the answers lay. He didn't have a scary scenario here with diseases and such, because it was a fairly closed society.

He was at the party for about an hour, meeting a few new people and getting to know everyone better. There were as many women as men. He was talking with a beautiful girl named Yvonne when he realized that fact. He was talking *with* her. They hit if off very well. Juli saw it, and told him to ask her to come to the house. They would leave in a little while.

Juli took Earl home, and Lenny took Yvonne. In the morning, he was even more confused because he felt much the same about Yvonne as he felt about Jon. It was the freedom and lack of silly pretenses.

Freedom. He'd never known it before – and hadn't known that he hadn't known. He was with Yvonne because they both wanted it that way. He was with Jon because they both wanted it that way. He cared for both of them. Deeply.

He stayed in bed until the sun was actually coming up, in the morning. He slid out of bed, not waking Yvonne, and went into the kitchen, where Sandi had set four places. He told her Marko hadn't come home.

"I know. It's for you and the pretty girl and Juli and Earl."

He nodded, and went to have a quick refreshing swim, then rinsed in the shower and went in to wake Yvonne for breakfast. Juli and Earl came in while they were eating, and they decided to go, the four of them, for a cruise.

"Don't fish!" Sandi warned. "We don't have room for anymore!"

They all laughed, and took their time getting ready, then went out on the boat. Each couple spent time in the cabin of the boat while the other couple swam or explored a small island. It was a wonderful day!

When they got back, Marko was just leaving to go into town with Selene. She and he hit it off better than even Juli thought they would.

Yvonne went home, and Earl went home. Lenny nor Juli wanted to go into town, so they stayed at the house. Leon and Sandi came to watch a movie Juli bought on DVD. They went to bed about midnight. Juli offered to sleep with Lenny. Sleep is all. Things hadn't clicked enough between them to do more, and they both had enough sex to last one night! Lenny said, "Why not?" and they slept close together.

All they did was sleep.

In the morning, Juli said he was going to go to St. Elvan's for some things, and to meet with a couple of the people he knew there. Marko wasn't back, and Lenny was offered a chance to see the island, so he went with Juli. They went around the island a bit together, then Juli had the meeting. It was business he was handling for his father, so Lenny could fend for himself. They would meet at five at the dock, then head back to Tintada.

St. Elvan's is a lot different than Tintada. It's more "modern" and "civilized" – which means it's more a tourist trap. Lenny walked around and bought a couple of shirts and a bright bathing suit. It was just four, so he went into a small café to waste the time. He was there for about ten minutes when a dark bullish man came to sit across from him at the little table. Lenny had seen him several times around town, but hadn't so much as nodded.

"Marko Ponti?" he asked.

"No. Lenny Hamilton. What do you want?"

"May I see some identification"

"No. What do you want?"

"I'm Don Kagan. I'm with the FBI."

"So?"

"I want identification! Now!"

"Go fuck yourself. You have no authority here. Get off your high horse and tell me what you want. I'll either answer or tell you to fuck off. One more demand from the big bad FBI agent and I tell you to fuck yourself, on general principles."

Kagan studied him for a minute. He didn't say anything.

"Waitress! This man is bothering me!" Lenny called to the waitress.

"Okay. You win that one," Kagan said. He flipped open a case and showed Lenny his FBI credentials. "So? I already said I know you have no authority here. What do you want?"

"I was told Marko Ponti was on that boat you came on. I know that other one isn't him, because I've been here before, and he was. I was supposed to go to Isla Tintada, but they won't let me in, and are an independent country, in a sense. I don't know what happened. We used to get along with them.

"I have to find out what Ponti is doing out here."

"Marko and I are on a vacation. He's not doing anything – and Dubya happened. I'm surprised you're allowed anywhere."

"Not Marko. His father."

"I doubt he even knows Marko's here. This was done with the Howards and me, mostly. They invited us to stay here while they're touring Europe. Julian is their son. He's there, and we're palling around together, is all. Marko has a girlfriend he's with today."

"No shit? It's important."

"No shit. Marko doesn't approve of the way Pops, as he calls him, makes his. He's loyal to the family, but not to the business. He's staying out of it."

"You can't stay out of it if you're part of the family."

"You can if Pops is the head of the organization, and pulls all the strings. This isn't Sicily, and this isn't nineteen forty."

"You known Marko long?"

"Since we were fifteen. Five plus years."

"I wish I could believe you. It could be very important to Marko."

"I'm not in the habit of lying."

"Okay. Tell him there's something funny going on with that place, and we don't know what it is. The Howards dropped out of a clear blue sky and landed on that island. We don't know where they got the money. They have over six billion dollars in offshore banks, as far as we can trace. That's a lot of money not to have a source. We wonder how Ponti's connected."

"Julian's used to living like he is. The Howards used to live on Martinique before coming here."

"How did you find that? We can't find anything before they moved here!"

"I know some people who worked for them in Martinique."

"Maybe that'll be a starting point. I'm going to be real disappointed if they're legit. I've put in a hell of a lot of work on them, already."

"C'est la vie."

"Yeah."

Juli was walking by, and saw them there. He came in, and Lenny introduced Kagan as an FBI agent who was trying to trace his family. He laughed, and said there wasn't much to trace. Certainly not the FBI. They weren't from the states. He'd been born in Southern France, but his folks had a place in Italy, and one in Sweden. They were from Hong Kong.

"Hong Kong! What the hell...!"

"The metals exchange Dad founded is there. It was there thirty five years ago. That should be easy enough to trace.

"It's none of your business. We don't have anything to do with the US, except through the companies that deal with us."

"Then your parents are British?"

"What? You deaf? They were born in Hong Kong. Their parents were British and Swedish."

"Crap! I've wasted six years chasing somebody who doesn't have anything to do with me? Crap!"

He got up and stomped out. Juli got the giggles. "He'll waste another six years trying to get a connection through Hong Kong. He won't do the obvious and check their passports. That would tell them all they have to know, none of which is any of their business."

"Check their passports?"

"Mom and Dad are touring Europe. They have to present their passports, everywhere. Even I would be able to figure that angle! Get their passport numbers and check back on your handy-dandy Tandy!

"I guess there aren't anymore Tandy. I started out on one that was in a closet in the house in Martinique.

"Ready to head back?"

"Yeah. That was one strange encounter!"

"Yeah. With a non-FBI agent."

"I wonder who he is and what he's up to – oh! What was that about a metals exchange?"

"That's where we got ours. Dad and his father and uncle opened a precious metals exchange. They were sitting on eight or ten million ounces of silver when the US took it out of the money. It went from one sixty an ounce to eighteen bucks in a week! They sold it, and were paid in gold, so hit it richer and richer as the gold market went through the roof.

"Why?"

"I was snowjobbing some snobs in the bar on Tintada. They were oh-so-filthy-rich and had never met the Howards. Where did they get their money? I said, first, it was vulgar to talk about money and, second, that your family had a few million ounces of gold in a Mexican bank or something such. I think she pissed in her pants."

He laughed. He also said it was true, if not in a Mexican bank. Their own.

They got back to the house after dark. Marko and Selene were there, and Sandi said she would fix them something to eat. Juli said they would go into town and get something at the restaurant. It had been a tiring day, so they would come back early. He and Lenny cleaned up and changed clothes, then they drove into the town. They had a very good night, and went back to the house at about eleven thirty. Juli brought a man named Javier home with him, so Lenny would sleep solo. He giggled at the thought that he'd even think of such a thing.

He decided to catch up on his e-mail, seeing it was a bit before he usually slept. He noted his computer was warm, but didn't much care. If Marko was using his, the girlfriend might come in to use that one.

It wasn't off, it was on standby. He brought it online, and noted the last window was opened to Gmail. He clicked on it out of curiosity. It wasn't logged out, and the homepage came up – with "Welcome back, moonmaiden2154!"

What was going on? moonmaiden2154 was a woman Marko had introduced online, back in the states. Lenny thought she was from Modesto, California! This was very, very strange. Something was definitely not right, here!

He heard the bathroom door open and quickly went to Yahoo! mail and his own server. Selene came in, and said she was using the computer earlier, and may not have logged off properly, and was just checking to be sure she hadn't screwed anything up. She seemed very nervous. Lenny said he was just checking his e-mail.

More than one used the computer, and they didn't meddle with anyone else's stuff. She laughed, and said she would just be sure she wasn't still logged in somewhere, and he let her sit at the comp desk to quickly go to Gmail and log out – when she thought he wasn't looking. He could see her in the mirror.

"I guess I didn't leave it on anything! 'Nite!" she said, and went back into the bathroom.

Lenny sent a few pictures and a note that he had found a true paradise and was living a new way here. Eat your hearts out, you poor slobs who are stuck in the same dull place as always! He sent it to a list of people, including moonmaiden 2154.

He went to bed with a feeling that something dark and mean was hiding in the shadows. He didn't sleep as well as he had since he'd arrived on Isla Tintada. Too many coincidences weren't coincidences. That phony FBI agent, and now this were two too many to be real. The Howards and his being invited to this paradise under those conditions were pushing it. Was the woman the pilot brought not long before them Selene? This was over the edge.

Things were great, and he was in paradise. The idea there was a sinister purpose behind it was scary. He met the Howards online, which was probably real. Knowing Juli and Leon and Sandi was real. He wanted desperately for Jon and Yvonne to be real. He didn't trust any of the rest of them.

Was Hedges real? What was going on, there? Were the Pages real? There were supposed to be two more of the type on the island. If the Bushes didn't fit and were run off, why were those still here?

Reality was about to smack him over the head. He could feel it.

Well, they made a bad slip when he found out about Selene. It told him to not trust Marko for one more second. He would watch for a sign to tell him what was up. He would be as ready as he could be, so maybe it wouldn't work for them.

He felt he could trust Juli. He also felt he should warn him. It somehow involved his parents.

Okay. Filthy rich people who met the son of a gangster on the net, and were wheedled into inviting him to their home for a vacation when they weren't there. That had to be contrived.

Another thing to consider. What the phony FBI agent said might be very true. Being in a gangster family didn't have any way out. That would mean that Marko was working for his father.

Put it together! The Howards were among the richest of the rich, Ponti was a gangster who was known to scam rich people out of millions. Ponti's son had set this up. DUH!

It wasn't going to work, if he was in any way necessary to their plan.

What was the purpose of Kagan?

To find out what Lenny Hamilton knew or guessed. He'd played that hand perfectly – by accident! He was just being honest. He was just being himself. He didn't know or guess anything.

Then.

He got up at the usual time. He was going to stay in character, and act like nothing in the world bothered him. He would see what the next move was, and who would make it.

Javier and Juli came into breakfast on the lanai. Sandi had ham and eggs with toast, and a half cantaloupe for each. They chatted about various things until Juli suggested they take the boat around to town. The person who handled who came to the island wanted a meeting among several of the island's residents to discuss the selling of the Hedges place.

Already? It was just yesterday that Hedges decided to sell!

"Oh, there's a list of people who want to come here," Juli said. "Maybe he knew some of them, and told them he was selling. I doubt anyone he would recommend would be welcomed here."

They lazed around for an hour or so, then went for a swim together, then rinsed and went to the boat to go around. Nobody here dressed for anything. Nobody would probably care if they went nude.

Well, the Pages.

Before they went to the meeting, he and Juli, Lenny took Juli to the restaurant where they had a cup of coffee outside at the little table there where he'd met Jon. He said he had something he felt might be important for Juli to know, for his parents to know. He explained everything, what he feared, and what he thought. Juli nodded, and said his folks were a bit naive about some things. He made a long phone call, speaking in French, then said to come on to the meeting. He could delay anything, if that turned out to be part of anything.

"What I'm more interested in is that you were brought out here, expenses for everything paid. In the group my folks hang with, that wouldn't happen. We all have one hell of a lot more than we could hope to spend.

"Marko gives me a hundred twenty five when we got here, and will give me that every Saturday. There's no place to spend it here. Everything is paid, everywhere. It doesn't make sense to me."

"I can't think of what he's after. Getting close to my folks won't get him anything. They'd have to know him fairly thoroughly before they'd do any kind of business with him. A check of who his parents are would pretty well put a screeching stop to anything in the near future."

"It's something we have to learn. I don't have a clue as to how to do that."

"You've learned a hell of a lot more than they thought you would, already," Juli replied, dryly. "I think we should just go along, acting like we don't have any reason to suspect anybody of anything. Maybe that's what you're here for. Nobody suspects anyone else of anything on this island. If you're here for, what did you say? Four months? You wouldn't be under suspicion of anything. You're a very open and accepting personality. Marko isn't.

"Oh, he tries to act like it, but it doesn't ring quite true with him. I saw that and introduced him to the gringa in there with him, or so I thought, because they're a pair.

"I'm good at sizing people up, in some ways. I knew you'd go for Jon, and I knew he'd go for Selene. I knew her for less than a week before, and him for two days, and had that figured. I knew Jon for years, and you for a couple of days, and could figure that.

"I have a business acquaintance on the family, and connections with everyone. He's trained by NSY and Interpol, so knows how to get information fast and accurate.

"Let's go see if there's some connection with this meeting. I'll also say I felt you would make Hedges face himself, if you ever met. He's impulsive enough that your odd philosophy would get to him. He's insecure, and not able to think a thing through for himself, and he wonders if he's gay. I can tell that, because he seems to avoid me, while being fascinated with me. He's also a little jealous of my suggested appeal that means I've never slept alone for a night since I was twelve.

"That's because he has no friends, and probably never has had any. He can't understand ... anything. He's not gay, but he's not secure in that, so he has doubts.

"I didn't think you'd get him to move. How did you do that?"

"He was already decided, it was a matter of when and where. I just let him know that he was just prolonging a bad situation, here, so should try to find a place where he fit. After all, he told me he didn't fit, the first thing. He decided his only chance was finding the place he fits. He wants a family, and that would never happen, here."

Juli nodded. They went to the little community building, where some other gringos were sitting around, chatting. The Pages stiffened sharply when Lenny walked in with Juli. The Stevens welcomed him warmly. The Jensons were a middle-aged couple who seem pleasant enough, as was Francis Bellows. They chatted for a few minutes before the Kilmers came in. It was like when Hedges came into the bar. The mood of the place changed, immediately.

A few nodded to them, but no one spoke. They went to the Pages, and were soon in some kind of animated argument, or something. They didn't get loud, but there was a lot of arm-waving and hard looks.

Freddy Winton, the spokesman for the council, talked a minute with Juli, then Lenny was called over and introduced. Winton didn't mince his words. He said he wanted to thank Lenny for getting Hedges off the island. It would be greatly appreciated by most of the rest if he could work that same magic on two other couples here, then they would have a truly ideal community.

He called the meeting to order, and explained that Hedges had put his place on the market yesterday afternoon, and would be off the island within the week. Hedges had asked that he tell them all that he wasn't what he appeared to be, here, but it was his own fault. He wished all of them well.

"I have an offer for the property for him. It is for a great deal more than he would expect, but we all know there is no price to meet the value of the place, to most.

"The person who wants to purchase the place is here now, a guest of Julian Howard. I understand that he is of a family who would not be welcomed here, under any circumstances, but he is not like the rest of the family, and wishes to escape them and their influence. He has met a woman here he wishes to marry, which is part of the appeal of the place.

"He says that Mr. Hamilton will tell us about him. They have been close for many years, and Mr. Hamilton knows exactly how sincere he is."

He looked at Lenny, and nodded.

"This is all totally unexpected," Lenny began, thinking a mile a minute. "I, uh, would only have one question, at this time, if I were considering such as this speech or of, uh, recommending Mr. Ponti. (There was a gasp from someone.)

"Marko, I don't know how to say this, but, well, has no money of his own, so how could he buy the place without the family financing it? What would it mean, in the future, if he was indebted to his father to such an extent? Would the father be able to foreclose on a loan or something, and come here?

"I am not saying one word against Marko. I am wondering is ... all."

Juli winked, and nodded. The people chatted among themselves for two or three minutes, then Winton said, "Julian, what do you suggest? That is one salient point we must consider. I will tell Mr. Hamilton flatly that no one comes here we don't want here, so we could keep the father out, though it could lead to a nasty confrontation we would very much prefer to avoid."

"Why not postpone a decision for, say, a week? We can investigate, and make a decision based on information, not conjecture," Juli suggested.

"Second!" Page and Bellows shouted.

"Accepted. One week. Here. Adjourned."

Everyone stayed and chatted about mundane subjects, except the Pages and Kilmers, who soon left together. Bellows came over to be introduced. Winton joined them, to say, "Thank you, Mr. Hamilton. I had some suspicion that such a thing might be. We all thank you for your insight."

"It's Len, and I didn't know that Marko was involved in this. That was just something that occurred to me while I was speaking. I was wondering why he didn't tell me he was going to do such a thing. I think it could be more serious than you suggest, considering that those two couples are still here."

"And he isn't my guest, he's a guest of my parents," Juli said. "Lenny might not want to say anything negative, but I already felt that he doesn't fit here much better than Hedges did. I've had suspicions about Selene Forbes, his girlfriend, since she came here. She doesn't fit the culture. I think it might be a good idea to investigate her, as well."

Winton nodded. Bellows said he could find out a few things, fast. He used an agency in his business that was as good as existed investigating people. Juli said he had put his agency on it ten minutes before the meeting started, at Lenny's suggestion. It was too strange to just accept at face value – by a parsec!

When they got back, Marko asked where they went, and why. Juli said it was a meeting of the council to determine whether or not he and Selene could buy Hedges' property.

"Oh. I wanted to talk to Lenny about that. I didn't think it would be this quick, and I'm sorry if it put him on the spot."

"It won't make any difference, in the long run. They'll investigate their own way, but Lenny just said he couldn't say one word against you, that you told him often how you wanted to escape your family."

"That's all I ask. That he tell them how I really am. I didn't even consider living here before I met Selene. I fell like a ton of lead for her, and she feels the same about me. I never met anyone close to being like her before two days ago, now I'm in love, and have I got it, bad! This is a paradise for both of us! Thanks, Lenny!"

"Yes. All they want to know is how you really are, not what people think you are because of your family and so forth.

"They won't give a decision for another week or so, but you're here for a couple more months, so that shouldn't be any problem. I can see plainly enough that I shouldn't include you or Selene in any of my parties, or such. I'll consider that you're already married, and on your honeymoon, so won't want any side action. I think Lenny and I are close enough now that we can find plenty to occupy our time among my friends, here."

They all laughed. Marko said for Lenny to be careful. Juli's friends would probably try to seduce him. Lenny said they already tried – and were successful.

"Well, we would be in the way, here, so I'll move in with Selene at the place she's staying. The people are great, and wondered why she didn't bring a companion, or find someone here. We said we were made for each other, and waited, because of that. We waited for the perfect match."

"Oh! Maybe I shouldn't have told her about the whorehouse we stayed in in Kingston?" Lenny asked, innocently.

"If you'd told her about that, I'd already be a bloody pulp, laying in the street! I'll get my stuff together, and one of you can drive us to town?"

"Yes. Lenny can. I'm going to rest awhile, and get ready for town tonight," Juli said.

Marko quickly packed his things, and called Selene, who was in a gazebo by the sea, to get her stuff. Lenny drove him and Selene to town. He asked Marko if he'd let the Howards know he was leaving, and did that mean he had to go?

"I suppose you can stay as Juli's guest. You seem to hit it off. Is he the one who seduced you? Huh? Pant pant!"

"No, but I did sleep with him. It was nice, but we only slept."

Marko shook his head. "I didn't expect an answer! Cripes!" Selene giggled.

He dropped them off at a place just before town, and returned to take a long swim and rinse. He cooked the dinner, making a pork curry pizza. It was sort of a revenge. Marko wouldn't get any.

He went to town with Juli, and had another great night. He saw Yvonne, but she had to leave a bit early because she had to go to Dominica to see her aunts and uncles. She would be back in two weeks. The boat left Isla Tintada at three thirty in the morning, and arrived at Dominica at nine thirty that night.

He spent the night with a girl named Sylvia. She was a lot of fun, and made it known that fun was what tonight was about, nothing more. Lenny said nobody owned him, either. It would be great!

It was.

Juli told him the next day he could stay as long as he liked. Outside of the island, he hadn't met ten people in his life he got along with so well. He could spend the rest of his life there, if he liked. He said he didn't have a pot or window, and he definitely wouldn't stay as a bum, living off of them. He would stay a few more days.

"Oh, I think we can work something out. You might have saved billions for us. It won't be like you didn't earn it. We can get along very well, and I'll have someone to tell my deepest secrets to. Now all I have to do is have a secret!"

Life rocked along in its slow pleasant pace for three more days, then Juli got a report from his agency. It was about Selene Forbes, first.

Selene Marie Forbes (MP nee Forbini), born in Detroit, Mich. lived in New York, Chicago, Lansing, Carmel, Los Angeles, Modesto. No record. Secretary Gianini Group N.Y., Chi. Representative Bendetti Group, LA, Crml, Mdst. OUKN.

"I can figure what most of it means. What is OUKN?" Lenny asked.

"Other activities unknown. No records or people to interview. She was mostly a loner."

"And she worked for two different mob families, I take it, as a secretary."

"Looks like it."

"Connection with Marko?"

"Not here. Maybe Gianini, through his father."

They got a call from Bellows later, and went to see him. He had a report on Marko. He had been a lot of places for short periods. He was in Hong Kong with his father, six years ago, and again, three years ago. Father trying to buy gold when the bust came, and again, later. Possibly tried Howard Exchange, but didn't do business with them. There was a hint he was asked to remove himself from the property because of a suggestion to one of the minor partners. Howard Exchange was never, in any way, involved with underhanded, unethical practices. Draw your own conclusions.

He was in Modesto, with Pops, three months ago, and was seen dating a secretary for a suspected mob company. Her name wasn't known, but they had a few pictures at parties where they appeared with others. The copies of the pictures weren't the best, but it was Selene.

"I figure Ponti met ... no. Ponti went to that company to suggest a scheme having to do with precious metals. He was thrown off the property, but had checked the assets. The company had literally millions of ounces of gold bars. He determined to get it.

"The standard types of dodges to get the gold wouldn't work with Howard. They investigated him all the way, and he's as clean as anyone in the business, and cleaner than ninety nine percent of them. They found the Howards had recently moved from Martinique to Isla

Tintada. They tried to come here, and were flatly refused.

"How to get a hand into the Howard fortune? There didn't seem to be a way.

"Then their son, an apprentice mobster, met a man who was corresponding with the Mrs. on the web, because he collected and worked with driftwood art, her favorite hobby. They were soon becoming actual friends – so the junior mobster inserted himself into that and played a game where he became a confidant of sorts with both of them. He managed, by some subterfuge, to have himself invited to their place on Isla Tintada. We don't know how he was able to do that or why he brought the confidant along.

"We don't know if he somehow manipulated the thing with Hedges, but his girlfriend was here two weeks before he and friend arrived.

"Things were going well when Julian Howard came home. Marko is able, in ways, so managed to ingratiate himself there, also.

"Hedges, the sale, the scheme to get some property here, close to the Howards. We aren't sure if he manipulated that or just grabbed an opportunity.

"Something. Selene Forbes is staying at the Gardner place. They are in Belgium, have been for two months, and won't return for three more. They have discussed selling the place, because it interferes with his medical needs. He has an arrested cancer that demands he stays close to the medical facilities near Brest. I'm not in the least certain the Gardners are aware Selene is there. Where the scheme was to go after they got the property is anyone's guess."

"They would know, from earlier, that the council would have the say, as to them coming here," Juli suggested. "They would have to get here some other, more indirect way. There are hundreds of ways to have a person under medical treatment agree to something they don't know they've agreed to."

"So. How do I figure?" Lenny asked.

"I'll find out. Tonight," Juli replied. "We can have the meeting, on schedule. I'll suggest we invite Marko and Selene to join us. We can be most pleasant to them until then, no matter what we actually feel. Their best strategy will be to stay low profile and out of sight until they have the place sewed up."

"That's what we'll do, then," Bellows agreed. He called Winton and made the arrangements.

"Well, we're almost in town now, so maybe I'll use Jon's computer to find what we need to know from Mom," Juli suggested. "I'm curious as to how he worked her, and why Lenny, thank whatever gods may be! is here."

Lenny and Juli went to Jon's place. Lenny met the wife, and was a bit nervous, but they acted as always. Jon even hugged Lenny a bit long and close when they arrived. Lena didn't seem to notice.

Juli explained that he needed to use the computer. It would be an ungodly hour where his parents were, but it was important.

Jon had Skype, so Juli was able to talk. She was using the computer when he called, and answered. They spent a couple of minutes in mother-son idle chatter, then Juli asked her exactly why Lenny, driftawoodwaytwenty, was there. It was on speaker.

"Lenny? He was the one I really invited. Marko wanted to give him a great birthday present, and I had told him about the place, and that I wouldn't be there, so he could surprise our friend with a vacation in paradise. I don't believe I would have invited Marko, otherwise. We're not so close. We don't really have anything in common."

"Well, Marko is with a woman, and isn't here. Lenny loves the place, and we've become very close friends. I want to invite him to stay with us. He fits. He fits the island. He fits with the natives and with us, except the assholes. He convinced Hedges he should leave."

"He's welcome for as long as he wishes to remain. I hope you two have found something. I worry about your penchant for promiscuity. It's dangerous."

"He's worried because he isn't among the wealthier classes. He thinks he would owe us. He's doing something I'll tell you about when you're back home. It will save us billions. It's a scheme he uncovered. He wants to find a way to pay his own way."

"Well, if he can produce driftwood pieces as fine as the ones he sent pictures of to me, he can make a great deal more than he can find use for, plus he'll be doing the thing he loves. I will expect instructions when I'm there."

"Mrs. Howard? I'm Lenny. If the pieces in your lanai here are your work, perhaps *I'll* request instructions from *you*!"

"Oh, go on, silly! I think we'll be great pals, if you're anything like on the net."

"Mom, you know the Gardners. Could you find out if they know they have houseguests?"

"Houseguests? Of course not! Nita would never allow anyone in her house when she's not there!"

"Do you have a number, or anything, so I can contact her? Bellows would greatly enjoy throwing those people in jail in Jamaica!"

"She's flowerdowagerforty at hotmail dot com. I was chatting with her yesterday."

They chatted for another twenty minutes, then Juli e-mailed Mrs. Gardner. She said she hadn't invited anyone to her house, and had no idea anyone but Hilda and Frank, who kept the place for her, were there. There was a short wait when she said she had to check with Norman, then she returned and said he might have said some woman could go there to look at the house, as a realtor. He didn't remember clearly. Juli thanked her, and said the people would be thrown out and possibly incarcerated for being there.

"Well, we can have our meeting and handle this," Bellows agreed, when they reported.

Juli and Lenny went back to the house, cleaned up, decided not to go anywhere, and watched a movie on the big set, cuddled up together. That led to more. It was a very pleasant night, for both of them.

"Everybody have a seat," Winton called. "This is a formal meeting with a secretary and all that rot."

Everyone moved to the chairs. Marko and Selene were toward the right front. Marko gave a thumbs up to Lenny, along with what looked like a smirk.

"We are here to decide about selling the Hedges property. I've turned the investigation over to Bellows, so he'll take over, now."

Bellows stood, and went to the small lectern to check a few papers there.

"I've done a fairly complete investigation of the suggested buyer, and have discovered the following.

"As we all know, Marcus Aurelius Ponti is the son of a world-infamous thug and gangster. He has never done one thing to deny that. He, in fact, states it plainly, and claims to be trying to escape that life and business.

"He came to this island, ostensibly to housesit the Howard place. He claimed to have an agreement under which all expenses would be paid, in addition to a weekly stipend, to him and to Leonard James Hamilton, who most of us have come to know and respect.

"I say ostensibly, because we, as could only be expected, contacted Mrs. Howard. She told us there is no stipend, and that the invitation was for Len, with Marcus as second. A birthday present for Len. Len did not know this, though he has been greatly puzzled as to why he was brought along, at all, and why to housesit a place that had a live-in staff."

"What the hell!?" Marko cried, jumping up.

"Sit down!" Winton ordered.

Bellows continued. "Be that as it may, they are here, and have become quite popular, certainly Len.

"Things change, in life. Whatever the plan was, perhaps Marcus wanting a vacation in a place where his parents would not come, Marcus met with Miss Selene Forbes, spent his time with her, and claims to have fallen in love, so wants a place here to live in peace.

"That is what you claim, Mr. Ponti?"

"Yes (contritely). I'll admit I misstated some things, but, as you said, things change. I met the perfect woman for me, and want to get away as far as possible from my family."

"I see. You never knew Miss Forbes before?"

"No. She was a delightful surprise!"

"I see. Then why do we have these pictures of you with her from Modesto, California?"

He jumped up again, looked around, then sat to stare at the floor.

"As to the lovely Miss Forbes. She is staying at the Gardner place, lately with Mr. Ponti. The Gardners were not aware she was there, much less him.

"Mr. Ponti, I would appear that you and your father have cooked up some ridiculous scheme to place into use here. In doing so, you have broken the laws here. By international agreement, you will face those charges here, but will be sent to Jamaica for your incarceration, for which, by that agreement, we'll pay.

"The law here says that lying before the council is perjury, and that you will serve up to two years for each count. You are convicted of two counts, by your words today. I will, as judge, sentence you to two years incarceration in Jamaica. I'm sure you will not enjoy the stay there.

"Miss Forbes, you are illegally entered and occupying a domicile here. The law is the same if it is a native or a resident. Two years. You will be sent to Jamaica, also.

"If that is all? My wife and I have a dinner date."

"Move to adjourn," Winton called.

"Second!" from several.

"Oh! One other thing!" Winton said. "Mr. Ponti and Miss Forbes, the boat will be here tomorrow to transport you to Jamaica. It leaves the dock at five twenty in the morning. Be aboard with all your possessions, or you will be held in lockup until the next boat, Wednesday. Consider that we need not feed you or offer any amenities, if you are convicted of criminal acts. I can assure you, certainly, that you would much prefer Jamaica." He turned, shook a few hands, and left. The other people filed out until there were only Juli, Selene, Marko, and Lenny left.

"Does he really think I'm going to get on a damned boat to Jamaica tomorrow morning?" Marko spat. "He'll find out who I am!"

"You're a two-bit two-faced half-assed thug," Juli replied. "You're less than nothing here."

"Well, what about *him*!" he demanded sourly, pointing at Lenny.

"What about him what? He's here as a guest of my mother, and has always conducted himself exemplarily."

"But ... he can't stay here if I go! He won't have a penny to his name!"

"He'll have the reward for stopping you. I think Dad will want him to have a reasonable reward. Say the Hedges place and a couple of million dollars to spend. Maybe he can move in with me. We get along, and I know two women and several single men who would welcome him. If he gets tired of one, he will be welcomed at the next. The council can declare him a citizen, and he can stay as long as he lives, so long as he doesn't turn into something like you."

Marko looked like he wanted to cry. He raised a fist and swung at Juli, who ducked and flattened him with a hard right to the jaw. "You have enough to contend with now, so I won't charge you with assault and add a year. Get it through your thick skull that we don't do things here like you do in the states, and that you are *not* bringing that here."

"Marko, you were just using me, after pretending to be a friend. I don't – didn't – have many friends. I have to thank you for bringing me here, but I don't owe you the time of day, because of *why* you did that. I'm home, and I'm free. I care about most people here, and believe they care about me. You'll never know that, and you'll never be free. I find that very sad."

"Pops'll have me out in an hour! Selene too! This is all horseshit!" He stood shakily.

"Maybe, but you've had a taste of paradise, and will know that you've arranged it so that you never will have another. I pity you, for that," Juli said. "You can now spend the rest of your life knowing that you've given that to Lenny, while insuring you can never have it."

"Pops can buy me my own paradise place!" he snarled.

"Nobody can buy you paradise," Lenny said, sadly. "It has to come from inside. You don't have it there."

Marko looked glumly at the ground. Selene was looking mostly scared. Lenny and Juli left. Outside, Lenny said, "You father is not giving me any reward, and definitely not buying the Hedges place for me!"

"I know. That was to point out to the shithead that he could have had paradise, but chose to refuse it. Lets go home to *our* paradise, Len," Juli said.

"Our inverted paradise," Lenny corrected.

"Whatever. It's still paradise!"

There wasn't any argument to that.

C. D. Moulton's works are available on most major outlets as printed or e-books. CD writes the CD Grimes, PI mysteries, the Det. Lt. Nick Storie mysteries, the Clint Faraday mysteries, the Flight of the Maita science fiction series, books on orchid culture and many others of many types. Mystery, adventure, intrigue, science fiction, fantasy, paranormal, mild erotica, and factual.

www.ingramcontent.com/pod-product-compliance
Lightning Source LLC
Chambersburg PA
CBHW050601160726
48003CB00002B/998